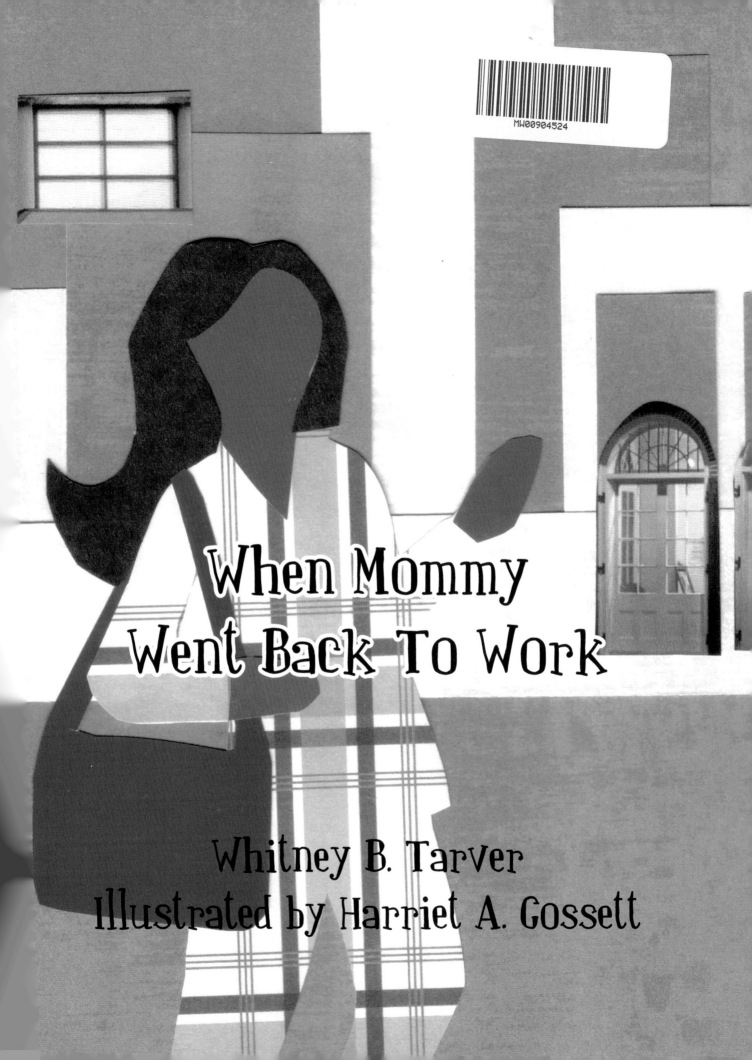

When Mommy Went Back To Work

Whitney B. Tarver

Illustrated by Harriet A. Gossett

 www.trafford.com

North America & international
toll-free: 1 888 232 4444 (USA & Canada)
phone: 250 383 6864 ♦ fax: 812 355 4082

Dedication

To my mom, Vivian, affectionately known as "Bibe", for sacrificing your career to be a "stay-at-home" mom.

To my grandmother, "Mutha", who has always been an inspiration to me, and exemplified what it meant to be a working mother.

To every woman who had to go back to work, even when she didn't want to. You are to be celebrated.

To my three children, mommy loves you.

Mommy has always been with me.
When I was born,

When I learned to sit up,
When I learned to crawl,

When I grew my first tooth,
When I first started to walk,
Mommy was always there.

Mommy says
she is going back to work
I asked her what that means

She says she will not always be with me like before.
This makes me sad.
I don't want to be away from Mommy.

Mommy says I'm not her little baby anymore.
I'm her big boy now, and big boys have to learn independence.
I asked Mommy, "What is independence?"

She says independence is when
big boys learn to tie their own shoes,
brush their own teeth,

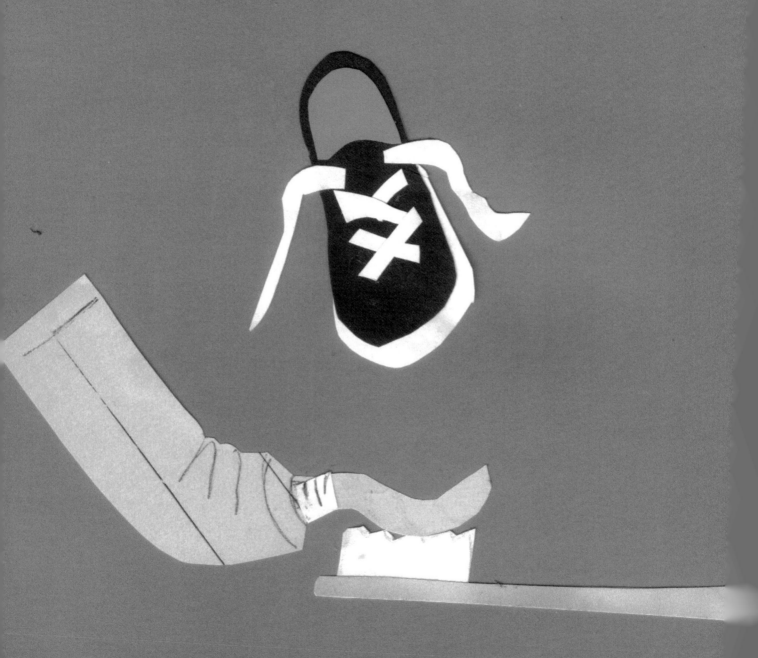

dress themselves,
use the potty,

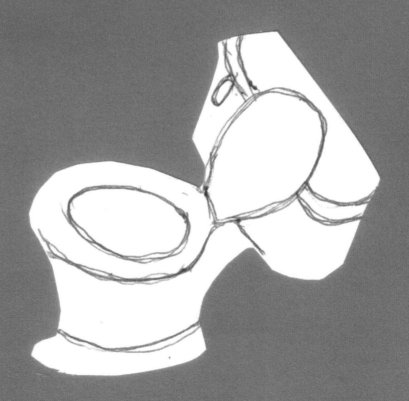

And pour their own milk
with maybe a little help
from their mommies

Mommy says I won't need to be
by her side all the time.
She says I will be going to daycare.
I asked Mommy, "What is daycare?"

She says it's a fun place for children
to go when mommies and daddies work.
Mommy says I'll make friend
with the other boys and girls ther

It makes me scared thinking about being
away from Mommy.
Mommy says it's okay to be scared.
She says she's even scared about
going back to work too,
but we must be brave together.

I feel better knowing Mommy and I can be brave together. Even though I won't be with Mommy all day like before, I know everything will be alright. Why?
Because I'm a big boy now!

CPSIA information can be obtained
at www.ICGtesting.com
Printed in the USA
LVIC030217140112

263866LV00004B